This Little Tiger book belongs to:

Campbell

_____

Christmas 2018 .

For Imogen, with love ~ P. B.

For Charlotte, Imogen and Oliver, with lots of love x ~ H. G.

If You Meet A

LITTLE TIGER PRESS LTD,
an imprint of the Little Tiger Group
1 Coda Studios, 189 Munster Road, London SW6 6AW
www.littletiger.co.uk

First published in Great Britain 2013 • This edition published 2017
Text copyright © Paul Bright 2013 • Illustrations copyright © Hannah George 2013
Paul Bright and Hannah George have asserted their rights to be identified as the author
and illustrator of this work under the Copyright, Designs and Patents Act, 1988
A CIP catalogue record for this book is available from the British Library • All rights reserved
ISBN 978-1-84869-795-9 • Printed in China
LTP/2700/2506/0918
4 6 8 10 9 7 5

DINOSAUR

Paul Bright   Hannah George

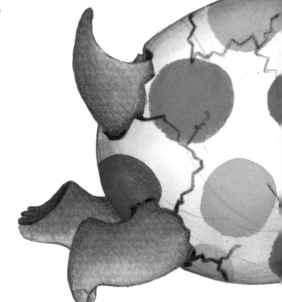

LITTLE TIGER

LONDON

Down in the valley
where the dinosaurs play,
Meg Mummisaurus laid an egg one day.
Great Grannisaurus said,
"I think it would be best,
To keep it snug and safe
in a dinosaur nest."

So Meg put her egg in a nest by the lake,
But Waggosaurus came, with a SWAGGER
and a SHAKE,
Wobbling the egg ...

For it's big, **big**, **big**, is a **Waggosaurus** tail –

As big as a **bus**, or a **boulder** or a **whale!**
If you meet a **Waggosaurus** you must tell him, without fail,

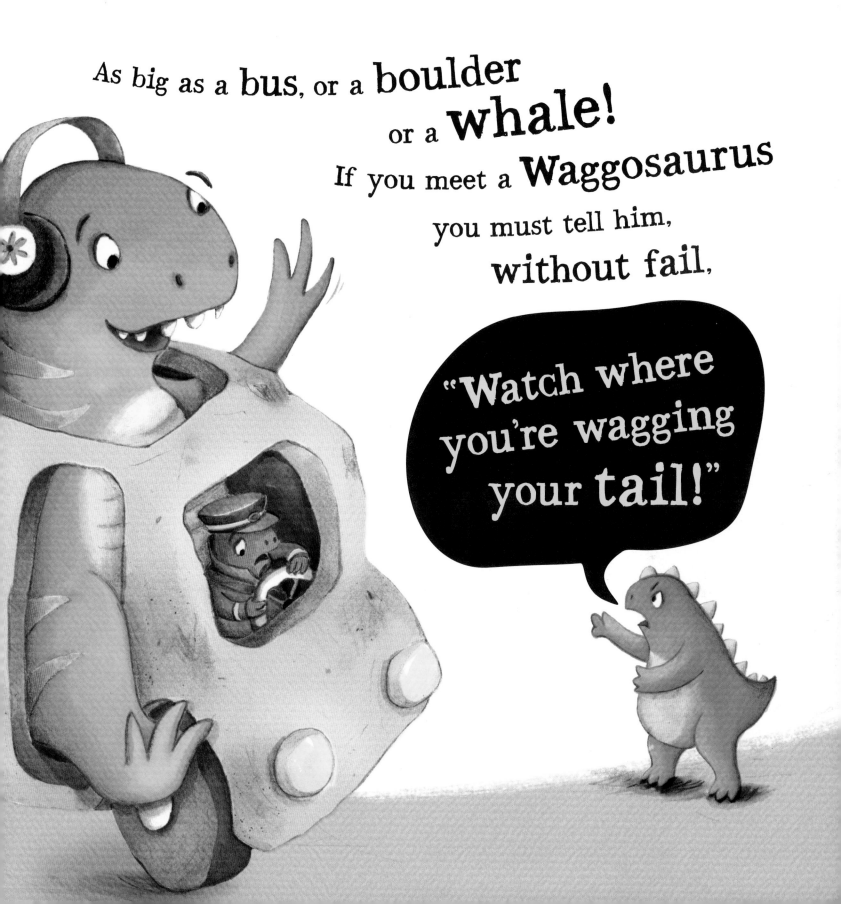

"Watch where you're wagging your **tail!**"

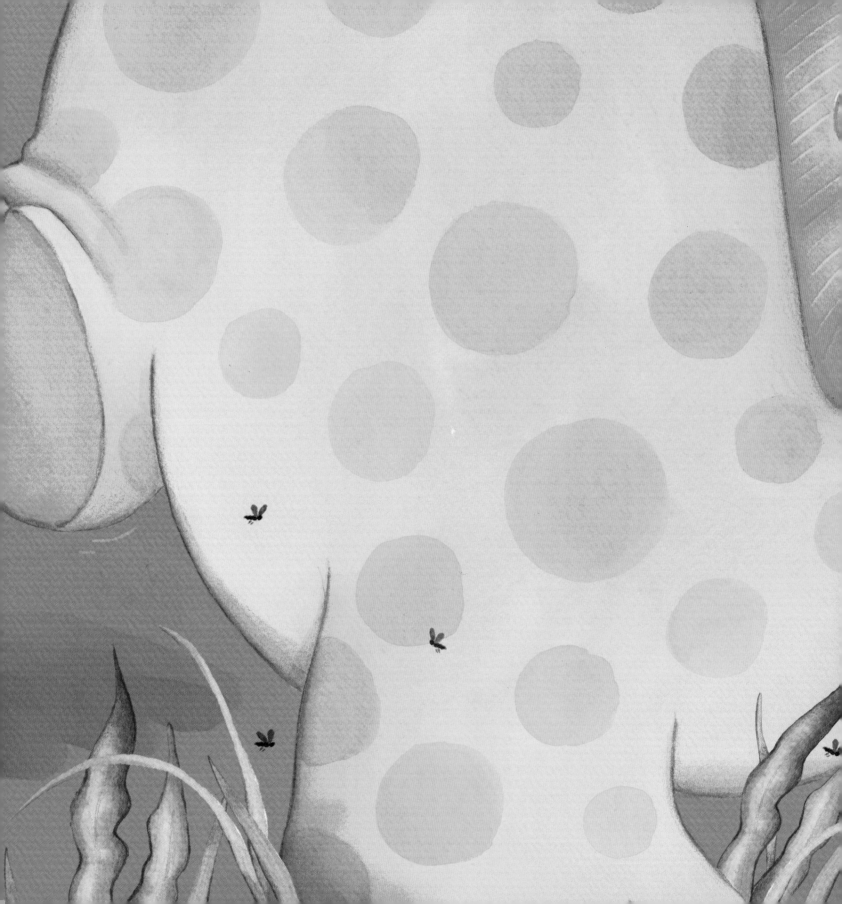

For they're big, **big**, **big**, are **Clomposaurus** feet –

A **Clomposaurus** ballerina
you will **never** meet!

If you see a **Clomposaurus**
come **stomping** down the street,

Shout . . .

"Watch where
you're putting
your feet!"

So Meg put her egg where
the green grass grows,
But Noseysaurus came,
with his snuffling nose,

For it's big, big, big, is a Noseysaurus snout,
And should he **start** to **sneeze**,
you don't want to hang about.
If you know a **Noseysaurus** …

Now every **Mummisaurus** needs a snooze or a snack, So **Meg** checked her **egg**, then she said, **"I'll soon be back!"**

And she went for a walk
by the swamp and the lake,
But that was a big mistake!

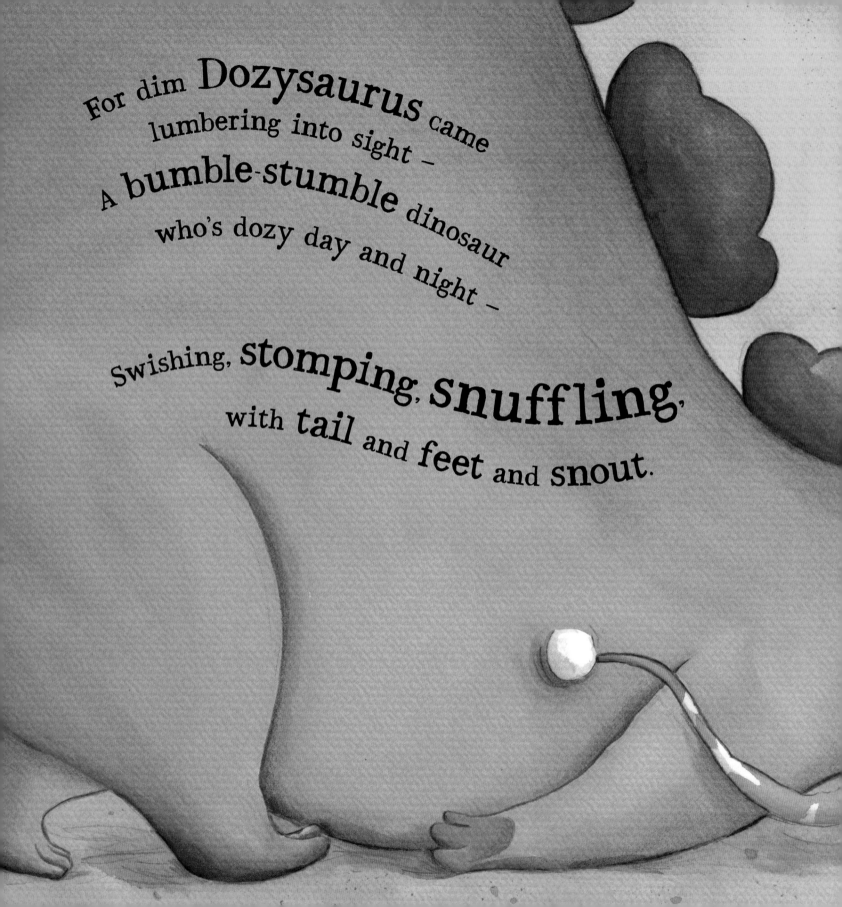

For dim Dozysaurus came
lumbering into sight –
A bumble-stumble dinosaur
who's dozy day and night –

Swishing, stomping, snuffling,
with tail and feet and snout.

Come back, Meg!
Protect your egg!
Look out!
Look out!

Look out!

and the **egg** gave a
crack.

Then the **egg** gave a
crick,

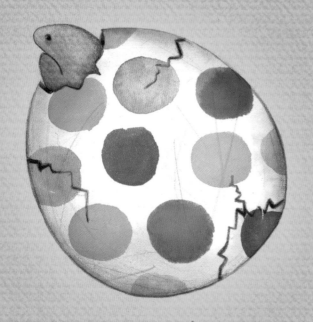

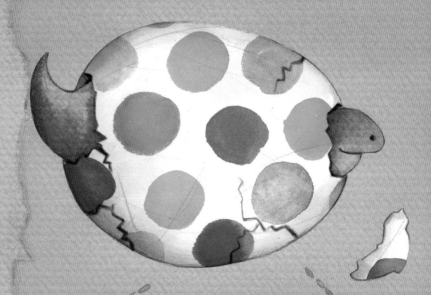

A **snout** poked
from the front end
and a **tail** stuck
out the back.

The **egg** stood up,
it gave a

SQUEAK,

and then began
to run!

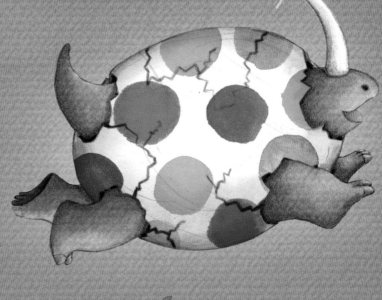

Crickle,
crackle,

came four feet,

emerging one by one.

"Ouch!" said Noseysaurus, rubbing at his nose.

"Ouch!" said Clomposaurus. "Could you mind my toes!"

"Ouch!"

said Waggosaurus.
"That's my tail,
you know!"

"Run!" said Meg.

"Run, little egg! Go, Spikisaurus.
Go!"

Down in the valley
where the dinosaurs play,
Baby Spikisaurus grows a little more each day.
And all the other dinosaurs say,
"Play just where you like, but...